SWEET REDEMPTION
A BBW & MILITARY ROMANCE

LANA LOVE

LOVE HEART BOOKS

Copyright © 2022 by Lana Love

All rights reserved.

No part of this book may be reproduced in any form or by any electronic or mechanical means, including information storage and retrieval systems, without written permission from the author, except for the use of brief quotations in a book review.

For more books by Lana Love, please visit my Amazon page at:

https://www.amazon.com/Lana-Love/e/B078KKRB1T/

or visit my website at:

https://www.loveheartbooks.com

❀ Created with Vellum

CHAPTER 1

CLAUDIA

"Come on, Claudia," Betty says from behind the reception desk of the dog shelter. She gives me a look that tells me to say yes. "Let me set you up with one of Walt's friends. I think you'd like this guy he works with..."

I look at Betty, not sure what to say. I love her dearly, but she doesn't get it when I say I don't want to be set up with some guy her boyfriend knows. I prefer the company of dogs to people. I don't trust people enough to let them close. I've had a lifetime of being let down. I'm tired of getting hurt. Dogs don't let you down.

"Maybe," I finally reply. If I go on a date with one of these guys and it's awkward and bombs, as it inevitably will, maybe she'll understand I'm serious when I say I'm not interested in dating anyone. She means well, and I like her, but I wish she'd respect my boundaries.

Betty's eyes immediately light up like she's already picking the dress she'll wear to my wedding.

"Don't go buying a wedding gift just yet," I laugh, grabbing Dixie's leash, the dog I'm walking today. Kneeling next to the elderly beagle, I scratch behind her ears. "You ready for your walk, old friend?"

"Dixie is such a heartbreaker." Betty's voice fills with sadness as she looks at the beagle. "She's been here the max amount of time. We can't keep her."

I knew Dixie had been around for a while, but I didn't realize she was reaching the limit for being adopted. It breaks my heart to see all the older dogs that people barely look at when they come in. Everyone wants puppies, then abandon them when they realize how much care a dog needs. If I had my way, no one would be able to surrender a dog for that reason.

"I'd take her if I could," I sigh. My apartment manager doesn't like that I have one dog, and I know he'd pitch a fit if I brought home a second, even if Dixie is a sweet and gentle old girl. She sleeps, eats, and loves. "I wish I could take them all home."

Betty looks at me warmly, her hand resting on my shoulder. "You have the biggest heart of all our volunteers, Claudia."

"One day, I'll have my own land, and then I can open the dog refuge." The shelter is overflowing with dogs. It hurts my heart when dogs are turned away because some will inevitably have to be put down. Sorrow crushes my heart as I think of the dogs whose lives are cut short through no fault of their own. I want to provide refuge for all of them...and one day, I will.

Shaking my head, I put a smile back on my face and hide how deeply this all affects me.

"It's a good plan, Claudia," Betty says as she turns to answer the phone.

I catch her eye and motion that I'm taking Dixie out for her walk. Pushing through the door of the shelter, I step out onto the street before Betty can get off the phone and start pressuring me to date someone.

It's not that I don't want a man in my life, because I do. It's been hard enough to trust other people, and after two bad relationships, I don't see myself trusting a man with my heart anytime soon. To say my last two relationships ended badly would be an understatement.

Dixie tugs at her leash, her interest in a tree the most urgent thing in the world. I smile and give her more lead, watching as she sniffs with serious intent before squatting and adding her scent to the tree.

As we walk down the street, Dixie looks up at me, panting. Her eyes are full of pure love and affection, making me happy. When everything else in the world is uncertain or unreliable, the unquestioning adoration of dogs fills my soul with loving contentment.

One day, I want a man who looks at me with the love and joy that Dixie does. I want someone who will support my dreams and goals and doesn't try to take from me.

But I realize that's probably too much to ask for, so I'm happy to devote my life to dogs.

~

"Oh, good! You're back!" Betty smiles.

"Just let me return Dixie."

I kneel in front of Dixie's kennel and take my time saying goodbye to her. As I'm about to stand, she puts her paw on my hand. A sob shakes my body. It breaks my heart in a thousand ways that she's overlooked because she's older and needs ongoing medicine. Not for the first time, I wonder if my landlord would throw me out if I brought a second dog home. He barely tolerates Midnight as it is, but Midnight is a charming dog, and even my landlord softens when he sees her.

"Can you stay around a little longer?" Betty asks.

"What do you need?" I ask cautiously.

"You know we work with Warrior Cares?"

I nod. Warrior Cares is a non-profit that helps military vets to readjust to civilian life. They have a program that places rescue animals with vets, and The Doghouse Shelter often works with them. When I have my refuge, I'd also love to work with them.

"One of their guys took home a puppy, and he's having problems with discipline," Betty explains. "Do you think you could help?"

"What's he doing for discipline? Does he know how to work with a dog?"

"I think his only discipline is getting frustrated and probably yelling at the dog." Betty sighs.

So many people adopt animals, especially dogs, and expect them to magically behave as they want. Dogs take patience and consistency.

My body tenses. "Do you suspect him of abusing the dog?" Nothing angers me more than animal abuse.

"No, not at all. I think he's frustrated and PTSD being what it is, he doesn't have the skills to cope with a puppy."

"Sure. I can help him out. I have time tomorrow."

"Too late, because he's on his way in now. I was here when he picked up his dog, and he's a hunk. Got a dangerous vibe about him. But in a sexy way." Betty grins and winks at me.

"Betty…" I close my eyes slowly to try and clear the not-so-obvious subtext that maybe *this* guy will be someone I want to date. I'm rethinking agreeing to this. I don't like that she's suddenly made it her mission to find me a man.

"You can't say no, because there he is."

"But I had plans…" I sigh in frustration. In truth, the plans are grocery shopping and taking *my* dog for a walk, which I could easily reschedule. But I hate being steamrolled, especially when Betty's motivation is more about putting me in the proximity of a single, sexy man than helping him train his dog.

I open my mouth to object, but my jaw drops as a tall, muscular, tattooed man walks into the shelter. Or, more accurately, he's dragged in by an overexcited Lab puppy. He's wearing a tattered Army jacket, which is well worn. When the man's eyes land on me, an alarm ricochets through my senses at the wildness in them. Betty said dangerous, but the zing of alarm and attraction that hit me makes me stumble.

I take a step backward, feeling incredibly off balance. My heart races, and my body flames with desire. How can a simple glance from this man have such an effect on me?

CHAPTER 2

GLEN

Mutt strains at the leash, pulling me with a force I didn't think a dog his size was capable of.

"I said NO!"

The women in the shelter gape at me, and a pretty brunette steps forward, her face flushed with anger. "You can't talk to a dog like that."

She has curves that make me nearly drop the leash. "Sorry," I say, holding up my free hand placatingly. "It's just... Mutt is a force of nature, and we do not speak the same language."

The bubbly woman who helped me adopt Mutt comes over, smiling and gesturing for the beautiful brunette to join her. My mind is already daydreaming about being alone with the brunette, but I blink rapidly. *You can't even handle a dog. What makes you think you can handle a woman? What makes you even think she would want you?*

"Hi, Glen! We can totally help you with that. Or, *Claudia* can." She turns and gestures toward the brunette,

Claudia kneels in front of Mutt, and he immediately calms and sits down.

"Son of a…" I mutter under my breath, stopping myself from swearing when Claudia looks up at me.

I see a mix of protectiveness and hurt in this woman. I instantly recognize the hurt. I see it every morning when I look at myself in the mirror. It's why I want to live a solitary life, but I've been having… anger problems, and Warrior Cares suggested therapy, which seems like a sissy-ass thing to do, but even I can admit it's working. My therapist said I needed a living creature to care for and who relied on me.

"He's young," Claudia says, standing and extending her hand to me. Her brown eyes are tense with challenge.

"Pleasure to meet you," I say, shaking her hand firmly. After years of being around men who view shaking hands as a competition of strength and dominance, I have to force myself not to grip her hand like I want to break it. What I want to do is pull her against my body and lose myself in her knockout curves.

"Glen, I'm sorry you came down. I can't help you immediately." Claudia turns so I can't see her face, but something passes between her and Betty. "I have plans this afternoon, but I—"

"Not to be pushy, but when can you help?" I cut her off, a surge of anxiety overtaking me. "I'm at my wit's end with Mutt here." I don't know how much more of Mutt I can take unless he starts behaving, which isn't happening right now.

"What's your dog's name?"

"He… I call him Mutt."

She looks at me like I said his name was Shit Stain. Mutt seemed like a fair name, but the look in her brown eyes tells me it's a terrible name.

"I haven't thought of a good name yet." A sudden need to please Claudia overtakes me – I want to do whatever will make her happy.

"Yeah, definitely choose a better name. I have plans today." She gives Betty a pointed look. "But I can help you out tomorrow. I understand how frustrating an untrained dog is, especially if you've never owned one."

"Is it that obvious?"

Claudia smiles, and it's like storm clouds parting to reveal a bright blue sky and blazing sun.

"Painfully. But I do understand. Give me your number, and I'll call you when I'm free. Is that okay? Do you have plans tomorrow?"

"No plans, no." Giving Claudia my phone number feels like offering her a promise. I haven't said goodbye yet, but I'm already looking forward to hearing her voice and seeing her again.

~

Whatever I thought my life would be after I joined the Army, this isn't it.

I'm a wounded vet, sitting in a rinky-dink apartment, watching Mutt run around with enough energy to make me weep. How is this a good idea?

You need someone to take care of that isn't yourself. No, not a relationship. I want you to get a dog.

The therapist's voice rings in my ears. As aggravating as Mutt is, he has his moments, and I see what my therapist meant. When he's asleep and his paws are jerking like he's running through a field chasing rabbits, something in my chest unwinds. It's the same when he jumps into bed with me at night. God knows I tried to keep the bed to myself, but the sound of his snores is soothing. I'm even getting used to waking up with him curled against my body. That's if he's not pacing around the bedroom, his claws clicking against the hardwood floor.

Mutt growls as he attacks one of my Army boots, and my blood pressure goes through the fucking roof. "Dammit, NO!" I yell at him.

He thinks I'm playing and jumps up to bite the boot I'm holding above his head. Remembering what my therapist said, I close my eyes and count to ten, reminding myself he's a dog. This is how a dog behaves – it's not intentional malice.

But when I open my eyes, he's chewing on the area rug I bought. A red haze clouds my vision, and I know I'm close to breaking. Reaching into my pocket, I pull out my phone and look at the entry for Claudia. I remember how pretty she is and for a split second, I forget about Mutt. Do I call her? We're supposed to meet tomorrow, but I don't think I can hold out that long without damaging something or taking Mutt to the pound. And something tells me Claudia wouldn't forgive me if I abandoned this dog.

"Hello?"

"Hi. Claudia. This is Glen. We met at the shelter today. I need… goddammit Mutt, what did I say? Son of a bi—. Sorry, I shouldn't swear with you."

Claudia laughs, and my heart does a pitter-pat I don't think it's ever done. "It's okay. I understand. Tell me, what's going on?"

"He's chewing everything. I gave him extra food, but he went after one of my boots, and now he's trying to demolish the rug I bought last week. I'll be honest, I'm seeing red and am…" I struggle to find the words so I don't scare her off, but nothing comes out.

"I understand," she says again, her voice softer. "You're overwhelmed."

"Yeah." I grit my teeth, trying hard as hell to keep it together.

"Okay. First. Do you have a water bottle?"

"Yes."

"Okay. Grab that, empty it, and put your dog and the bottle in the bathroom. Can you do that?"

The patience in Claudia's voice is a balm and helps to soothe me. She's not barking like my former CO, but she's giving me orders. Orders I can follow. "Hold on."

I put the phone down and head to the kitchen. I pull out a bottle of water and do as she says, then march back to my living room, where damn Mutt is still going at it with the rug. I pick him up by the back of his neck, and he flails as I carry him to the bathroom, where I put him down on the floor and toss him the bottle. The sound of crunching plastic is immediate as he works his jaws over the bottle. Closing the door, a small sigh of relief escapes me. I know it won't last long, but the dog is distracted, and my thoughts are not screaming.

"You still there?" The idea that she hung up spikes my anxiety more than I want to admit.

"Yes, I'm still here. Did you get him squared away?" Claudia's voice is calm and firm like she's had this conversation a thousand times.

"Yeah, he's making a racket with it, but better the bottle than things I care about. Is this a phase or something?"

"Partly, but he needs toys. He needs things to chew on. Don't give him food when he's like this. He'll probably eat it, but then he'll gain too much weight. That's another set of problems."

"Got it. Look. I was at my wit's end. I know you were chilly about helping me train Mutt, but can you help me? I have to figure him out, or he's going back to the shelter." The sound of her breath tensing fills my ear, and I don't have to be told she's upset. Meeting her a few minutes earlier was enough to know she loves animals and dogs. And as frustrated as I am with Mutt, I don't like the idea of abandoning him. "I want to make this work, but I need help."

Admitting I need help so easily is a strange feeling. In the Army, we're taught how to fall in line and obey orders. We're brothers in arms. Asking for help from a civilian, especially a woman, doesn't come easy. It surprises me that I instinctively trust her, but I do.

"Promise me you won't give up on him." Her quiet voice wavers.

My heart constricts. There's so much emotion in her voice, and I recognize the sound of decades-old pain. "Ma'am, I give you my word. I just need your help."

Claudia chuckles unexpectedly. "Okay. I'll help you. On one condition."

"Anything." As I say the word, I know I would do anything for her. No questions asked.

"Don't call me ma'am."

CHAPTER 3

CLAUDIA

Midnight and I are almost at the park to meet Glen when I spot him ahead of us. He's a hulking guy, his muscles bigger than I remembered. He looks big enough to break out of his clothes if he moves the right way. I can't deny that imagining him losing his clothes sends ripples of desire through me I've only experienced when masturbating.

Glen and his dog are waiting at a crosswalk, Mutt straining at his leash and nearly walking into traffic multiple times. I'd believed Glen when he called me at the end of his rope, but I didn't realize how untrained Mutt is.

Glen says something to Mutt, which I can't hear, but I see the frustration rolling off him. "Why can't you behave!" he suddenly yells, his voice harsh.

A woman at the crosswalk looks at Glen in alarm, clutching her purse to her chest and taking several steps away from him. Glen says something to the woman, holding up his hand in a peace gesture. She's clearly not buying it.

"This was a bad idea," he grumbles as I come up behind him.

"No, it wasn't," I say, placing a calming hand on his arm.

His muscles flex tightly, but when he looks at me, a rush of something comes over his face. He seems happy to see me.

"He's testing your boundaries," I explain softly.

Our dogs sniff each other and dance around as they say hello. Midnight is an older rescue, but nothing in this world could force me to give her up, not even my evil landlord.

"He's testing my ever-loving patience is what he's doing." Despite being mad at his dog, Glen stands up straighter as we talk, and if I didn't know any better, I'd swear he was puffing out his chest at me.

That can't be right. Why would he think I'm interesting? He just needs help with his dog.

Still, I can't ignore the warmth building inside me from being close to him again. Obviously, he has demons, but when he looks at me, I feel safe. It's confusing as hell, but I feel like I can trust him. This is a strange feeling, because I haven't trusted anyone – truly trusted anyone – since I was a little girl.

I shake my head, willing myself not to get lost in fantasies of Glen or old, painful memories.

"Light's changed," I say, tilting my chin toward the traffic light. "We should get going before the rain starts."

∽

As I suspected, Mutt isn't a bad dog, but he hasn't had any obedience training and probably never had anyone tell him no. A pang of frustration goes through me. Was he someone's cute gift and abandoned when the owner didn't put in the work required to discipline him?

"He's done well," I tell Glen as we sit on a bench, watching our dogs run around the designated area in the park.

"Is he good now?" There's hope in Glen's eyes.

It pains me a little to break his bubble. "Ah, not really."

I smile at Glen, working to keep my tone firm, but not bossy. Everything has gone well today, but I can't entirely forget the outburst I saw back on the corner. Betty told me Glen's dog is through Warrior Cares, which I know means he probably has some PTSD. I know vets can go off like a live wire flying through the wind. I'm not sure how much I can trust him yet, no matter how much I *want* to.

"You mean we can do this again?"

Glen's voice has a different tone, like he hopes he can see me again. I have to admit the thought of seeing him again fills me with anticipation.

"Yes," I say, struggling to keep my voice even as my heart pounds. My mind is imagining spending more time with Glen – lots more time – but the list of reasons this can't work is long. "This isn't formal training, but a few more sessions can help you learn how to work with Mutt."

The sky rumbles and suddenly goes dark. Glen and I look up just as sheets of rain begin drenching everything.

"Mutt!" Glen yells as he stands.

"Midnight!" I call, trying to pull my coat around me. It flaps open as a gust of winds blows into us.

Midnight hesitates for a moment, then comes bounding over to me. Mutt follows her, overtaking her and jumping on me, his muddy paws landing heavily on me.

"Dammit, Mutt!" Glen's voice is sharp, but his face is apologetic when he looks at me. "Sorry about that. Are you okay?"

"I'm fine." My voice is tight as I look down at my favorite shirt because, yes, I tried to look nice for Glen today. Two big, muddy pawprints adorn the front of my shirt. I reach my hand to my chest but stop when Glen touches my wrist. His fingers send shockwaves through my body.

"You'll smear it if you do that." Glen's eyes flicker toward my chest. "I live nearby if you want to get cleaned up."

I hesitate before nodding. I'm anxious about being alone with him, not because of what he might do, but because of what *I* want to do.

∼

"Thanks," I say as I step out of Glen's bathroom, wearing one of his Army t-shirts. The fabric is thin and soft, and I tug at it to make it magically not stretch tight against my breasts. "I could've gone home." My voice trails off as I watch him put my shirt in the washing machine and start a cycle.

Well, I guess I'm here for the next two hours.

"I'm sorry, Claudia. You can see why I need your help."

My heart lurches when Glen turns and smiles at me. It's the first time I've seen him smile and something about it jolts me to my core. "It's not a problem. Mutt is a puppy – it's what they do."

I look at our dogs, half-heartedly playing with the empty plastic bottle Glen gave Mutt earlier. Mutt and Midnight slow down, their energy clearly spent, and before I can even blink, Midnight is curled into Mutt and snoring.

"Those two sure get along."

I nod at Glen, surprised. Midnight isn't antisocial, but she generally isn't interested in other dogs. With Mutt, it's like they're old friends.

"We got some time to kill. Beer?" Glen opens his refrigerator and holds up a couple of beers.

"Sure."

"So tell me how you got into dog training." Glen returns to his living room, handing me a beer and settling onto the other side of the couch.

"Well, I'm an accountant by day. Working with dogs is a passion of mine. As for how I got into it…" I hesitate. I don't normally talk about the real reason, but the urge to tell Glen surprises me. "I had – well, *have* – a difficult relationship with my family. The short answer is that things were tough and being a girl in my family wasn't easy. My dad was in and out of jail, and my brother is as difficult as my dad." I take a deep breath. "It's hard for me to trust people – really trust them – but dogs are easy for me. I understand them. Does that make sense?"

Glen is slow to respond, but his eyes are dark when he does. "Yeah, it does. My dad was rough on me. Nothing was ever good enough for him. I ran wild after I escaped high school, but…" he pauses, taking a deep breath. "I nearly died from some fucked up shit a friend got me into. Had the timing been different, we'd have ended up in prison. It was one of those moments of clarity people talk about. I figured the Army was a better option, and maybe it'd straighten me out, so I enlisted. I didn't have much common sense, but I had enough to realize I was on a bad path, and it was either make a change or get used to prison."

"I understand wanting to escape," I say, my voice quiet. "I want to save all the dogs. I'd love to work with a program like Warrior Cares to help veterans like you. My dream is to save enough to buy some land so I can open a dog refuge."

Mutt comes over and curls up next to his feet, and Glen reaches down to scratch his ears. I'm not sure he realizes he's doing it.

"What about your family? They still in the picture?" Glen asks.

I fold my arms across my chest, tension rising in me as I think about my brother. "It's just my brother and me now, but we're… we're not close." No matter how much I try to hide it, I know my disappointment is raw and obvious.

Glen raises an eyebrow. "That's too bad." He takes a long drink of his beer.

"Yeah, it is. But I like dogs, and I'm good with them. Honestly, they're easier to deal with than people." I take a sip of my beer and try to put on a happy face. Some people look at me like I'm crazy when I say I prefer dogs to people, but Glen nods like it's the most natural thing in the world. "What about you?"

"I think my childhood was similar to yours. Parents are gone now. The Army was my family, but…" Glen's eyes cloud and he balls his hands into fists. "I'm still close with some of the guys I served with. Others... others can rot in hell. Pardon my language."

"It's okay." My phone buzzes in my jacket pocket, but I ignore it. It's probably Betty checking up on me. She knows I was meeting Glen today.

I can't deny there's a connection between us, which has taken me by surprise. It's awkward to be with him in his home, but there aren't any red flags. He's troubled, but I don't feel in danger at all. If anything, he seems like someone who would defend me to the death, despite not knowing me.

"There's nothing like the brotherhood of the military," Glen says, his voice thick. "But I saw people doing things in the name of war that were shameful and cruel. It's not right to take advantage of situations and people like that."

He opens his mouth to say more, but his eyes close, and the struggle to remain calm is written all over his face. The emotion drains from his face as if he's locked it away somewhere. He rubs a hand on his arm, and I notice a network of scars only partially obscured by his tattoos.

I'm not a shrink, but I know the way he's shutting down and internalizing his feelings isn't healthy. It's the same thing that has me wanting to be a recluse running a dog sanctuary. *Though who am I to talk about internalizing pain?*

After a long moment, Glen looks up at me, his eyes filled with a raw vulnerability that makes me gasp. I see in him the same profound disappointment in the rest of humanity, and it stuns me. I knew other people felt like this, but I've never met one.

"Hey, it'll be okay. Not everyone is like that." I don't fully believe this, but I believe it enough to say to Glen and sincerely mean it. He doesn't look like he can handle this burden.

"That's what my therapist says." Glen opens his mouth to say something more, but his eyes move to my coat. "Are you going to get that? Your phone's been buzzing for ten minutes."

"You're probably right." I look at my coat and sigh. It's not Betty. No matter how motivated she is to matchmake for me, she's not this overbearing. It can only be one person.

"Hey, Joe. What's going on?"

CHAPTER 4

GLEN

"I'm busy right now. I can't talk." Claudia's voice is tense and her knees start bouncing uncontrollably. She stayed upbeat even when she was talking about her family and how difficult they were. But whoever she's talking to has her on edge. It's like all the joy has drained from her face.

I get up from the couch and pace in my small apartment, unable to control my tension and jealousy, but Mutt wakes up and starts dancing around under my feet, and I nearly step on him by accident. I order Mutt to settle down, but it doesn't do any good.

Hearing another man's name on Claudia's lips is a physical blow. The idea of another man's hands on her curvy body, of her in another man's bed… my body shakes from how crazy it makes me feel.

Maybe it was a mistake to believe she was single. She has a way about her that suggests she's alone.

I sit on the couch, inches from her, fighting the urge to hurt the man who is making her upset, as I will the call to end. She's a ray of sunshine, and seeing her like this is devastating. Someone like her shouldn't know the kind of pain I see in her right now.

The buzzer on the washing machine makes us both jump, and putting her shirt in the dryer gives me something to do. Mutt looks at me as I walk past, but thankfully he settles back down next to Midnight and doesn't cause another scene.

"You want me to come out there today? Joe, surely you can take care of this on your own. You don't need me to deal with this." Claudia's head drops, and I can hear Joe's voice over her phone practically yelling at her. Even without hearing what he's saying, his frantic whine of urgency is unmistakable.

After putting her shirt in the dryer, I walk toward Claudia and wave my hand to catch her attention. She looks up at me, and I mouth *is everything okay?* She shrugs and looks away again, and a rage I haven't felt since I was deployed boils up in me. I need to know what's going on, so I can fix things for Claudia. She is a sweet woman who doesn't need more stress in her life.

"But what about my dog, Joe? My neighbors are gone, and you know they're the ones I trust her with. Yes, yes, I know. What am I supposed to do with Midnight?" The words come from Claudia's mouth with a sharp bite "I'm sorry. Yes, I know you're allergic. Fine. I'll see what I can do. I'll call you when I'm on my way."

Claudia ends her call, puts her phone down, then leans forward, her elbows on her knees and her head in her hands. Her breathing is jagged for a moment. I give her space since I don't know what's going on, but pressuring her would be the wrong thing to do right now.

"I'm sorry," she finally says. "That was my brother."

I breathe a huge sigh of relief that it's not some deadbeat boyfriend of hers who is causing her grief. But I know family can cause you a deeper grief than someone you're fucking.

"What's going on? How can I help?" There's an energy in my body bursting to get out. I need to *do* something to help Claudia and possibly hurt this brother who so clearly hurts her.

Claudia takes a deep breath and looks at me. Her eyes are filled with a tension and sadness that pulls at my heart and makes me want to roar with rage.

"It's… it's a tough situation. My brother always seems to be getting into trouble and always turns to me."

"Do you help him out?"

"As much as I can. Most of the time. He wants money. But I don't have any to spare. Any extra I have is being saved so I can open the dog refuge I told you about."

I've known plenty of men and women like her brother. Always looking for a handout. Never wanting to earn their own money or work.

"Thing is, he's allergic to dogs. So I'll have to pay to put my dog up because the people who normally watch her are on vacation this week. I'd take her to the shelter, because Betty would take care of her, but they're already full."

"How long will you be gone?"

"I... don't know. Sometimes when he's like this, talking to him for a while will help him settle down. But there've been times I had to be there for a couple of days to help him untangle some mess he was in. I don't want to leave Midnight on her own, in case I don't come home tonight."

I take a deep breath. I'm not sure if I'm comfortable with this, but I want to help Claudia. "How about you leave Midnight with me? She gets along with Mutt here. I can handle two dogs for a night, even two nights."

"Are you sure about that?" Claudia raises an eyebrow and smiles.

The moment she nearly laughs, it's like happiness exploding in my soul. Pride surges through me at making her smile, even when she's so upset.

I know I have to be honest with her. "I'm not entirely sure, but I'm willing to try. Let me help you. I'll do anything I can to help you. I'm on your side."

Claudia looks at me for a long minute and then nods. "I appreciate this, Glen. But the moment you need me, I'm a phone call away."

"Everything will be fine, Claudia. I've got this. You go deal with your brother. And we'll all be here waiting for you when you get back."

∽

IT'S BARELY BEEN two hours since Claudia brought over food and instructions for Midnight, but I miss her already. Being with her calms my soul. I can see she's carrying her own set of wounds, but she's found a kind of peace I never thought I would find again. Claudia is showing me it's possible. She's grounded in a way the essence of my being craves.

Mutt and Midnight wake up and start running around my apartment, sliding across the wood floors and crashing into the little furniture I have. The sound of a lamp falling over sends a surge of frustrated adrenaline through me.

What the hell did I agree to?

I agreed to help out a beautiful woman, that's what.

"Both of you! Calm down!"

The dogs pause for a moment, but when nothing happens, they go right back to what they were doing before.

I look at my phone. Claudia probably hasn't even made it to her brother's place.

I pace around my apartment, frustration rising in me. The dogs aren't the only ones who need to release some energy. I grab their leashes and get them ready to go for a walk, trying to remember what my therapist told me. Take some deep breaths. Focus on something different. But it's hard with Mutt and Midnight running around. They have more energy than I expected.

My phone rings and I lunge for it, hoping it's Claudia. My heart sinks a little when it's not, but I'm still happy when I see who it is. We're in the same support group at Warrior Cares.

"Hey, Kirk, what's up?"

"How you doing, Glen? Just wanted to check in on you. Haven't seen you at group in a few weeks."

"I appreciate it, man. I'm not gonna lie. It's been hard." I exhale and sit down on the couch. Talking about things is against my nature, but it's slightly easier with Kirk and the other guys in the group because they get it. They've also lived through the shitshow that is war.

"You still going to therapy?"

"I am, yeah. It's helping, but you know I'm not much of a talker."

Kirk chuckles. "Yeah, I know what you mean. It works, though. Did you get a dog? I know you were talking about it."

"Yeah," I sigh, "Mutt here has been a pain in my ass."

"Hold up. You named your dog Mutt?"

"Yeah. It's not very original, but I'm not sure about keeping him. I had to get a dog trainer to help me because Mutt has a mind of his own."

"But it's good. Glen. You're trying, right? It sounds like you're trying."

"Yeah, although I think I'm more interested in the dog trainer than Mutt. He does have his good moments, though."

Kirk chuckles. "Tell me about this dog trainer."

I sigh and smile. "Claudia is something. She's kind of hard to read. And she's standoffish. But there are moments when she opens up, and I see the possibilities. When we have those moments, she makes me believe there are good people in the world. Because you know the shit we saw boots on the ground."

"Yeah, fucking war will warp your mind." Kirk sighs heavily.

"But how are you doing? You still in therapy too?"

"Now and then," Kirk says. "I mostly have things under control. And Colleen helps me when I don't. But man, I gotta tell you it's worth everything when you find the right woman. Do the work with the therapy because you don't want to hurt your woman. When Colleen got pregnant, I swear to God, it was like everything in the world made sense. Having a family man, it's hard work."

I listen to Kirk, and I have a tickle of an idea. But I don't know Claudia well enough. I mean, I like her, and there's something there. The idea of coming home to Claudia and our dogs makes me smile.

"You're gonna have a kid. I never thought I'd see the day. When's Colleen due?"

"You and me both, Glen. You and me both. Colleen is due in about five months. I can't put it into words, but knowing we're going to have a baby, I've never wanted to protect anyone as much as I want to protect our baby. And believe me when I tell you I would do anything to protect Colleen. But this... it's different. Like I said, I can't even describe it. But it's the most powerful thing, and almost dying in combat has nothing on seeing a woman carrying your child."

I smile as I listen to Kirk. I can't see him, but I can hear his smile as he tells me about Colleen and the baby that's coming. Will I ever have anything like he's describing? I hope so, but I'm not sure it's possible for me. I look at Claudia, and I want something with her, but I have a shit ton of baggage from the war. There's no reason any sane woman would consider taking me on. She hasn't seen the extent of my scars yet.

Mutt and Midnight race past me, and I hear yelping. Mutt is growling as he bites Midnight's neck. "That doesn't look like playing," I mutter.

"What did you say, man?"

"Sorry, Kirk. I've gotta go. These dogs are fighting."

"Wait a minute. Dogs, plural?"

"Yeah, I've got Claudia's dog with me. She had to go bail out her brother from some shit situation he's created for himself. I'm taking care of her dog."

Kirk laughs. "Yeah, man. It sounds like you're going down the same road I went down. Wasn't looking for love, and then it smacked me in the face."

"Whoa, now! It's a little bit early for that." I try to pass it off as a joke, but when he said it, I realized I wanted something more with Claudia. I barely know her, but I want her in my life for a long time.

"Kirk, man, I'll catch you later. I've got to figure out what's going on with these dogs. And I don't know what I'm doing. But if her dog gets killed, then I'm going to be killed."

CHAPTER 5

CLAUDIA

"Why can't you do this for me, Claudia?" My brother's voice is a harsh whine as he snaps at me.

The air in his small house is stifling, but there's too much tension to ask him to open the window. It would only cause another argument.

"I'm not going to give you any money. You know I'm saving money for the dog refuge."

Joe scoffs and rolls his eyes. "Oh, the *dog refuge*." He holds his hands up and makes mock quotes as he says the words.

"What's wrong with the dog refuge?" I know he's baiting me. I try to shut down my emotions, but I'm braced for the negative emotional impact of whatever he's going to say next.

"It's a pipe dream, and you know it, Claudia. You're never going to get it off the ground. Are you saying the dogs are more important than your family? Maybe you could eat less food?"

My mouth falls open when he criticizes my weight. I don't obsess over it, but it still hurts a lot when it's used as a weapon against me.

I look at Joe and feel nothing but frustration. He may be my brother, but he only calls me when he needs something – and "something" is always money. He never asks how I'm doing, but he'll insult me in multiple ways. He doesn't like dogs and thinks everything I'm interested in is worthless.

"If you're going to be like this, I'm going home. Insulting me won't make me help you."

I brace myself for a fresh wave of anger. Every time I try standing up for myself with my brother, he comes at me harder and stronger, wearing me down until I give in.

"Claudia," he says, his voice softer this time. "I'm sorry. My friend's got this business idea, and I know it's good. It's better than the other ones. And we'll get it off the ground and make so much money. Hell, I'll even be able to buy a dog sanctuary for you."

Joe's never been friendly or considerate, so when he says he'll buy me anything, especially something as big as the dog sanctuary, I know he's lying through his teeth. "Joe, I'm sorry, but I can't help you."

"Claudia." His eyes flare as he grabs my shoulders and shakes me. "You've got to help me. I know you've got the money. You're an accountant. You're good with these things. I swear I'll pay you back."

"Just like all the other times you've paid me back? I could have opened the refuge by now." I push him away from me and cross my arms over my chest. Anger vibrates through my body. Why can't I have a normal relationship with my brother? Why is everything always about him and trying to take things from me? "And being an accountant doesn't make me rich. It means I have a job that can support my life."

"I'm not letting you leave unless you help me, Claudia."

"What?" I step back in alarm.

Joe's face is scary and dark. There's something about it his expression that makes my skin crawl. I should never have come here. I should know better by now.

Claudia, why do you do this to yourself?

Because I always hope it will be different.

"Joe, come on. Why can't you get a job and figure it out on your own?"

"This is the job I want. I want to do this."

"Joe, I'm sorry, but I'm leaving now. This isn't something I can help you with." My body vibrates with tension as I walk across the room, pretending to be more confident than I am.

But Joe comes behind me and grabs my arm so tightly I know I'll have bruises.

"Let me go!" Pain makes my voice crack. I can't stand up to him physically, and he knows it.

"No, Claudia. Not until you lend me the money."

"Okay, let's talk about this," I say, backing down and playing the peacekeeper like I always have. My mind races to find a way to handle this, but I know he won't willingly let me leave unless he gets what he wants.

Relief and happiness wash over Joe's face, and he lets go of my arm. I rub it, wincing at the bruises already forming.

"I need to go to the bathroom, and then we can talk about this. Okay, Joe?"

"Yeah, sure. Fine. Sounds good." Joe's bouncing around his living room, like he always does when he gets his way. It's scary how he can jump from elated to intimidating.

I lock myself in the bathroom and wonder how I'm going to get out of this. Once you give an inch with Joe, he will take so many miles. I sit there with my head in my hands. There isn't anyone I can call for help. Betty would come, but it wouldn't help anything.

Glen.

Can I call Glen? I don't know him well, but I trusted him enough to leave Midnight with him. I don't have anyone else to turn to.

I pull up Glen's number on my phone and stare at it. Is this too much to ask? Would he even care? At this point, I don't have anything to lose. Except the dog refuge.

Joe's doors and walls are too thin for me to make a call without him hearing, so I send a text.

Hey, Glen. I hate to ask but I'm in trouble and I need help. Can you come?

I type in Joe's address, hoping Glen sees this and is willing to come.

Within seconds, he responds.

I'm on my way.

Joe is walking around telling me about this harebrained scheme of his friend's. And it sounds as terrible as all the others he's ever told me about. But he's so excited, thinking I'm going to give him the dog refuge money, he doesn't notice I've shut down. I don't say anything, just occasionally nod as I listen to his amped-up monologue about finally striking it rich.

I sit on his couch, arms crossed against my chest, counting the seconds until Glen shows up. I know Joe won't stand up to Glen. Joe is skinny, but Glen is tall and muscular, with an imposing presence. My brother will take it the wrong way and be even madder at me. But what can I do? I'm not giving up on the dog refuge.

I check my phone discreetly to see if there's a message from Glen. I turned the ringer off so Joe wouldn't hear it if he messages me again, but he catches me looking anyway.

"Got someplace else to be, Sis?" His voice changes from elated to menacing in the space of a breath. There's a snarl in his voice, making my skin crawl. *Please get here soon, Glen. Please.*

"I was checking the time," I say, trying to deflect his suspicion.

"There's a clock on the wall."

"Sorry, I'm used to looking at my phone." I muster a smile. "Tell me more about this business."

I don't normally lie, especially to my brother, but I can't help feeling a little bad that Glen is on his way over to help get me out of this. I wish I could stand up to my brother, but... it never works out that way.

What would it be like not to have Joe in my life? It's painful to think about, but the truth is it would be a relief. I want a brother, but Joe makes everything so difficult. He doesn't feel like a brother.

"Okay, okay. Fine. So when can you have the money to me? You can cover fifty grand, right?"

"Fifty-thousand dollars!" He's never asked me for more than a couple thousand dollars before. Even that's a lot of money, but at least it's manageable. There's no way I can afford what Joe is asking for, even if I wasn't saving to open a dog refuge.

"Fifty-thousand is a lot of money, Joe," I say, trying to keep my voice calm and low.

"You have it, Claudia. I know you do. You have a good job. You don't spend money on anything. He smiles again, turning on the charm, his hands outstretched in supplication. "Take care of your brother. Aren't I more important than the dogs?"

I inhale sharply and try to avoid his eyes. *Where is Glen?* The truth is, I care more about the dogs than funding another of my brother's harebrained schemes. "Joe, I can't give you that kind of money."

"You're not *giving* it to me, Claudia. It's a *loan*. I will repay you. I swear I will." He stresses every word so clearly that I know he's convinced this time will be different.

The knock at his door makes us jump. Joe goes to answer it, then pauses to look at me. "You called someone, didn't you?"

I shrink away as Joe opens up the door. He takes a step back when he sees Glen.

"Hey, Claudia, everything okay here?"

The relief of seeing Glen unwinds some of my tension. I suddenly feel like everything will be okay, and I won't have to give my brother an incredible amount of money.

"Hey, man. This is my house. I'm standing right in front of you."

"You must be the brother." Glen takes a step forward, his arms flexing. "Claudia, do you want to get out of here?"

"Yeah, Claudia is my sister. What of it? Claudia, who is this knucklehead?" Joe stands up straighter with false bravado, but I can tell he's intimidated. *Good.*

Glen's jaw clenches, but he ignores the insult and focuses on me.

"Joe, look. I'm sorry, but I can't help you with this. You'll have to find the money another way." I stand, a cold, nervous sweat breaking out over my skin.

"Can I suggest getting a job?" Glen says.

"Who the fuck are you to tell me to get a job? What did you tell him, Claudia?" Joe's voice is rising, and his cheeks flame with anger. "Why are you involving some stranger in my business?"

"She didn't have to tell me anything. I know Claudia. And I understand when she's in trouble. But I look at you and know exactly what kind of man you are. Or the kind of man you pretend to be. Claudia is coming with me, and you're not going to stop her. Do I make myself clear?"

"If you think you're—"

"If I think I'm what? Do you really want to challenge me?" Glen stands his ground in front of my brother.

The ferocity of his protectiveness takes my breath away. All my life, I've felt like an impediment to other people. No one has ever had my back. Our parents left Joe and me to fend for ourselves most of the time, and winning their attention and affection was an impossible challenge. The hurt of never being good enough for their support has followed me through life. I've spent so much time turning inward and trying to be as invisible as possible. But Glen… Glen sees me and his actions scream that he values me.

"Claudia," Glen says, turning to me and handing me his keys. "Why don't you grab the dogs and take them for a walk. I've got them out in the truck."

"I…" I look between Glen and my brother. Fury is written all over my brother's face, but I know he's unlikely to start a fight with Glen, if for no other reason than Glen is much bigger than he is and could probably lay Joe out flat in a single punch.

"I'm going to have a short chat with your brother. It won't take long. We'll be civil, won't we, Joe?" There are several levels of challenge in Glen's voice as he says this.

My mouth practically falls open when Joe nods his head tightly.

I leave my brother's house, my hands shaking from nerves. I believe Glen when he says he'll keep it civil, but I've also seen enough of him to know if Joe tries anything physical, Glen won't hold back.

Despite everything, I can't help but smile when I reach Glen's truck. I can see Mutt and Midnight curled up together and dozing through the window, each with a paw stretched over a rope toy.

It also makes me smile to see Glen learning to handle Mutt and give him what he needs to be a healthy and obedient dog.

They wake up when I open the door, and their energy rockets off the charts.

"Hey, hey," I laugh, warm love filling my heart as they jump up and vie with each other to kiss me and get pets. "Let's go for a walk and burn off some of that energy, okay?"

Locking up Glen's truck and putting the keys in my pocket, I grab the leashes for the dogs and head out. The weather is still a little cool after the rain earlier, but the sky is clear. The three of us walk around the neighborhood, and I let them sniff anything and everything, giving Glen whatever time he needs with my brother.

The more I think of Glen, the more I realize how much I like him. We both have difficult pasts, but we're trying to move past them.

"Hold on there." I tug the dogs' leashes to let a mom walk by with her kid and a bag of groceries, and it's a pleasant surprise to see that Mutt doesn't strain his lead. He's not sitting like Midnight, but he's not pulling the lead quite as much. He'll learn and get better.

Glen is casually leaning against the truck when we get back.

"Hey," I say nervously. "How did it go with Joe?"

"I believe we reached an understanding." Glen's voice is crisp. He smiles at Mutt, who's watching him and vigorously wagging his tail.

"Okay, that's cryptic, but it sounds like progress." I try not to get my hopes up too high, but I think if anyone can get through to Joe, it might be Glen. "Can I take you out to dinner? As a thank you? I know it's not fancy, but there's a food truck that makes the best burgers you've ever had."

As I hand Glen the leash for Mutt, an electric shock jolts me when our fingers touch. I look at him, wondering if he felt it, too. From the surprised look in his eyes, I'd say he did. Warmth builds in my core. *Could something develop between Glen and me?*

"That's the best idea I've heard all day. Lead the way."

CHAPTER 6

GLEN

"What did you say to my brother?" Claudia looks at me with awe as she wipes a napkin across her mouth.

"I had a man-to-man talk with him." I leave out the part about threatening him if he ever hurt Claudia.

"That's amazing. I've never been able to get through to him, and it didn't seem like anybody else could either."

I put my burger down. "I had a rough childhood, too. I understand what it's like. He's not much different from how I was before I joined the Army. He can still turn things around and not throw his life away. But if he doesn't change something, he's going to end ended up in prison or dead."

Claudia inhales sharply, her eyes widening in fear. "As you saw, we don't get along, but that's not what I want for him. I agree with you."

"Hopefully, he'll get on the right track. It might take a little time, but I also told him he can call me if he needs help."

"You would do that for him?" Claudia doesn't hide her surprise as she looks at me.

"Of course. I don't make it a habit to get involved in other people's affairs, but he's important to you, so I want to make that effort."

"I appreciate that, Glen. Thank you."

The smile on her face is genuine, and it lights up her face. More than ever, I want to wrap my arms around her soft curves and hold her close. I want to discover the pleasures of her body and make her happier than she ever imagined.

I put Mutt in my truck and walk Claudia and Midnight to her car. She puts her dog in the back seat and turns to me, a sweet smile on her plump lips.

"I don't know how to thank you for what you've done. It's more than getting me out of a bind today. It's just…thank you." Her voice chokes with emotion.

"Claudia." I take a step closer to her so we're inches apart. "I care about you. I want to help you, and talking to your brother was part of that."

Before I realize what's happening, Claudia wraps her arms around me and hugs me fiercely. "Thank you."

My heart pounds as I hold her tightly against my body. I want to see her let her guard down and also to let me show her how much I want her. She hugs me tightly, and my cock aches. Her body is so close, but I can't touch it the way I need to.

"Thank you, Glen," she whispers, her voice jagged.

She kisses my cheek, and a bomb goes off inside my heart. She begins to step away, but I don't release her from my arms. I lift my hands to cup her jaw. And then I do what I've been fantasizing about since we met. I kiss her on the lips. She freezes in surprise for a second, but then she returns my kiss with a passion that rocks me. I growl as I deepen our kiss and my body instinctively grinds against her.

We step apart. Her face is flushed and her eyes sparkle. I've never seen a more beautiful woman than Claudia. Deep pride fills me that I can make her feel this way and give her this happiness.

"I like you, Claudia. I do." There aren't words for all the emotions I'm experiencing. I'm drawn to her in a way I've never been to anyone, but it's more complex than that.

The light in her eyes changes. "I... I like you, too. I shouldn't have kissed you back like that."

"Did you like it?" I look at her, not comprehending. How could she kiss me with such enthusiasm and then pull back and shut it down moments later?

"I did like it, Glen, but I can't." The light in her eyes dies, and it hurts more than I could have imagined.

"We would make it work," I tell her. "Why wouldn't it work?"

She takes another step back and looks to the ground. Her voice is small when she speaks again. "It's hard for me to let people in. I'm sorry. I am."

The idea of losing Claudia terrifies me. I've developed a connection to her in a short time, and it's more powerful than anything in my life. With her by my side, we could achieve anything. But I know if a woman asks for space, you give it to her as a sign of respect.

"If I was out of line, Claudia, I apologize. But give me a week, and I'll prove you can put your faith in me. I promise you."

～

"Hey, how's it hanging, Glen? I haven't heard from you in ages. I know you're not calling for a cup of coffee and chat like a couple of grandmas."

"Yeah, it's good to hear your voice, too, man. You're still up on King Mountain, right?"

"Sure am. I don't think I'm ever leaving this place."

"Didn't you tell me you had some property up there, or a group of you bought half the mountain or something like that?"

"Yeah," Waylon says. "We do have a lot of land up here. You want to come live in the mountains? One of the guys is running some rentals and could use some help managing that."

"Possibly. I've got a friend who needs space, and I think your mountain might be the right place for her."

"What you got in mind?"

"Oh, yeah, we can make that work," Waylon says after I tell him about Claudia and the dog refuge. "You should come out here for a visit, see what we've got available and if you think it'll work. Bring her along, too."

"No. I'll come up myself. I want this to be a surprise for her. And I don't want to let her down if it's not going to work. Can I come out later today?"

I hear Waylon chuckle, but I can't help it. I have to prove to Claudia I'm different from anyone she's ever known. There isn't time to take it slow. The faster she's in my arms and my bed, the better the world will be.

"Yeah, no problem. I'll be here when you arrive. But I can tell you this. What you're proposing is a good idea. Ain't no one gonna fuck with you over it. You have my word. We'll keep her safe."

"Thanks, man. I appreciate it."

I PLAN to take some time off work so I can go and check out this abandoned cabin and land Waylon is talking about. He told me about how he's in a partnership with some other vets —all men who've decided that living in on a mountain is a better alternative to being a part of society. I get it.

Before Claudia, I might have gone up there and joined them myself. Staking out a cabin and spending my days alone doesn't sound like the worst thing in the world. Or it didn't before I met Claudia.

But the idea of living on a mountain with Claudia has a different appeal. If I spent the rest of my life with only her, that would suit me perfectly. I'm going to do everything in my goddamn power to make sure it happens.

I force myself to wait until I'm back in town before I call Claudia. I'm excited to share this with her and help her achieve her dream.

When I'm finally home, I feed Mutt, and he sits at my feet, cleaning his paws. Everything feels right with the world.

I pick up my phone and call Kirk. "Hey, man. Got a minute?"

"Sure. Hang on a sec." Kirk's voice muffles, and I hear him say something to his wife. "What's going on?"

"Ask me in a week," I chuckle, though the idea this won't work out… I can't even bear to think about it.

"Uh, oh. You okay?" Kirk's voice is alert, and I know he's weighing up if I'm in a crisis.

"Yeah, it's just…" I give him a quick rundown about what happened with Claudia. "I'm trying to set things up so she can start the dog refuge. You've said Colleen and the other lady do fundraisers for Warrior Cares. Do you think they'd do one to help out Claudia, so she can get things off the ground?"

Kirk chuckles. "You got it bad, don't you?"

I exhale and nod, even though he can't see me. "Yeah, I do. I'm taking a risk, but she's worth it. She's the one."

"I'm glad you've found a woman, Glen. You should talk to Colleen. Honey! Hold on, she's coming. You need any help with any of this, you let me know."

"Thanks, Kirk. I owe you one."

"Here she is. Keep me posted."

"Will do."

"Hi there, Glen. What can I help you with?" Colleen's voice is kind.

Without hesitation, I tell her what I have in mind and ask her if she could help. "What do you think? Could it work?"

CHAPTER 7

CLAUDIA

"It's nice to see you, Glen." I look at him, and my heart races. More than anything, I wish this was a date. It's been over a week since I saw him, and I haven't thought about anything other than our kiss and how amazing it was.

I wasn't sure if I'd see him again, but I didn't hesitate when he invited me to dinner. Being with Glen gives me a calm sense of safety, like he'll always stand up for me. He's the kind of man I think I could settle down with. Yet I know I wouldn't recover if I lost him, which makes the idea of opening myself up to him scary.

"So, what's this special thing you wanted to tell me?" I fiddle with the napkin in my lap. Alternately dreading and anticipating whatever he's going to say.

Glen takes a deep breath. "I know a guy who knows some guys, and I've done something. It's big, so I hope you don't get scared or overwhelmed."

"Okay." I look at Glen warily. "What's going on?"

"Well, you were talking about saving up to open a dog refuge."

I nod, wondering where this could be going. This man is a reluctant dog owner.

"Well, like I said, I know a guy who knows some guys, and they live over on King Mountain. They own most of the mountain, and my buddy told me they have a cabin with a plot of land that's been abandoned and needs fixing up. You'd need to finance any renovations, but they'll rent the place for pennies. Plus, he said if everything works out, they'll sell you the land, and it will be yours permanently."

My mouth hangs open as I listen to Glen. I pinch myself because there's no way this can be real. Things like this don't happen to me. I don't have luck like this.

"But where would the money come from? I don't have enough to start it on my own. It's not a cheap business to run."

"We've got that covered, too." Glen smiles at me with so much enthusiasm, it's contagious.

"We?"

"Waylon is going to help us with the cabin and the land. My buddy Kirk's wife hosts fundraisers, including for Warrior Cares. Colleen said she'll host a fundraiser to help you get the seed money to get things started. Colleen and the woman she's in business with are one-hundred percent on board with this." Glen smiles at me, but his hand is shaking as he lifts his drink to his mouth and takes a sip. "All contingencies are planned for."

I tremble, and tears build in my eyes. "Glen, are you serious?"

Glen isn't the kind of man who would play a prank, but I'm having a hard time wrapping my mind around this.

"I'm serious as a heart attack, Claudia."

"But why would you do this for me?" I understood Glen liked me, but this is… it's so far beyond anything anyone has ever done for me. It's generous and supportive and in no way a casual gesture to plan all this and get other people on board.

Glen straightens up in his chair and looks me straight in the eyes. With his attention focused on me, I feel like the most important thing in his world. "Claudia. I've got a difficult past. I've told you a little about why, but I didn't tell you that before I met you, my life was fucking bleak. Going to war and seeing the evil men perform, I didn't think there was any good in the world. I didn't think I could ever have redemption for what I've done."

My eyes fill with tears as I listen to Glen. He's been so stoic when we've been together, but I can hear the waver in his voice. He's letting me in. A voice in my head tells me I need to let him in, too.

"Claudia, getting Mutt was frustrating, and it didn't seem like he would make anything better. But my therapist suggested it, so I went along with it because I knew I needed something to pull me back from where my mind was going. I never imagined Mutt would become a permanent part of my life. But he brought me to you. And meeting you was a turning point in my life. You're sweet and honest and true. And you make me want to be the man I didn't think I could be."

My heart pounds in my chest. If I'm not careful, I'll start crying in the middle of this restaurant.

"You don't think it could work between us, Claudia. But I disagree. I passionately disagree. There's nothing I want more than to build a life with you and Mutt and Midnight and all the dogs we could help at your refuge. Being with you, Claudia, *is* my redemption. You're my second chance at a good life. I want to be by your side, supporting you and other vets like me who come back with a dark cloud over their heads. We can't save the world, but we can save a corner of it. What do you say, Claudia?"

Glen looks at me, and I can see he's trembling too. It took a lot of courage for him to say all this and open up to me. The future is expanding in front of me, and I'm scared but also excited. Glen is more than I ever dreamed I'd find in anyone, much less a man.

"Betty at the dog shelter is going to have so much fun with this," I say with a smile.

Glen cocks his head. "What does Betty have to do with anything?"

"She's been trying to marry me off to every single man who walks into the shelter," I reveal with a blush. "When she told me about you, she was ready to marry us off before I even met you."

Glen reaches across the table, and I place my hand in his. It feels safe and good. It feels like being loved. "Well then, we're gonna have to thank Betty, because she insisted I talk to you and no one else about Mutt."

"Yeah," I say. "I guess maybe she got this one right."

"I'd say so." Glen signals the waiter for the check. "Let's go to the mountain this weekend."

SWEET REDEMPTION

～

"THIS..." I gasp, looking at the land and the cabin Glen's friend Waylon is showing us. "It's perfect!"

I walk toward the cabin at the edge of a clearing with a sheer tree-covered incline behind it. It needs a lot of work, but there's plenty of space to take care of dogs and build a small barn.

Waylon crosses his arms over his chest and nods at me. "It's yours for the taking. Glen probably told you the place needs work, which I'm sure you can see. You take care of the renovations, and we'll negotiate a nominal rent for you. The guys and I can guarantee your safety. We don't get many problems up here, but..." Waylon pauses, and I see him debating whether to tell me something. "Suffice it to say there are occasional... issues, but we'll shield you from those. We'll put down our lives for you."

"I don't know what to say." I wipe tears of joy from my face, looking from Waylon to Glen. "But I say yes. Let's do this!"

～

WHEN GLEN SUGGESTED DRIVING over to King Mountain, I thought it was crazy. But I couldn't say no when he described what he'd lined up and how he would help me secure funding to get the refuge fixed up and the business started.

Glen was so happy on the drive up here that he could barely contain himself. It's humbling to see someone working so hard to make me happy. Little by little, I realize how much he believes in me and is committed to being my partner. He wants to help me achieve my dreams – not to mention he's sexy as hell. He's self-conscious about the scars he brought home after the mortar attack in the war, but I think they're a part of who he is. Most people hide their scars, but Glen's are out there for anyone to see. He's braver than I could ever hope to be.

"You warm enough?" Glen returns to our campfire, a heavy wool blanket in his hands.

"I wouldn't say no to sharing that. It's gotten chillier out here than I expected."

Glen sits next to me on the log and spreads the blanket across our laps as our campfire sparks. The sky above us is clear, filled with more stars than I've ever seen.

We sit in silence, an easy comfort between us. My mind still whispers that letting Glen into my life is dangerous, but my heart is screaming the opposite. I want nothing more than to give myself to Glen and start something amazing.

"You doing okay over there?" Glen puts his arm around my shoulders, and I lean into him.

"I'm perfect. Everything is perfect. Thank you so much, Glen. What you've done for me is out of this world amazing. I'm going to be able to help so many dogs." I look up at him and smile. It doesn't seem real that this is happening, but it's slowly sinking in.

"If you let me, Claudia, I'll be here with you, and I'll help you with the refuge. I don't ever want to leave your side. I want to learn about dogs, and I want to run this place with you. What do you say?"

I look up at Glen, and his face is heavy with anticipation. His arm is tight around my shoulder, but I can feel him trembling. He's given so much and done so much for me, and I can't imagine a future without him.

"If you're asking to be my partner," I smile at him, raising my hands and stroking his strong jaw. "Then I say yes. Unequivocally yes."

Glen lets out a whoop that echoes through the forest. In the distance, an owl hoots and flies across the sky.

Glen grins and pulls me close, kissing my lips hungrily. I open up and welcome his tongue as it probes greedily in my mouth.

Glen pulls the blanket off our laps and puts it on the ground behind us, away from the fire. He stands and pulls me up with him, tugging me against his body. My core is on fire with desire for him, and my heart is aching to give him everything. It scares me to open up to him, but I trust him. I know Glen will love me and do everything in his power to support me unconditionally.

"Are the dogs asleep inside?" I ask.

Glen arranged for us to stay in one of the remote rental cabins Waylon and his friends own. He said it would be a lot of driving to go back and forth from the city to the mountain in one day, but I knew he wanted to stay the night up here as much as I did.

"They are," Glen says, leaning in to kiss me again. "Door's closed good, so they can't get out." He kisses me again, and my knees go weak. "Come over here with me."

Glen leads me to the other side of the campfire, then spreads the wool blanket over the ground. He kneels on it, and I follow him. Soon, we're lying next to each other, our hands roaming and discovering as we kiss.

I bite my lip to stifle a moan as he sucks and kisses my neck, his hand moving over my hip and under the waistband of my jeans. I gasp and push my body toward him, desperate to have his skin against mine and to feel him move inside me.

I reach for his shirt, giggling in the night air as I struggle to unbutton it using only one hand. "Take that shirt off, or I'm going to rip it off you."

Without another word, Glen sits up and pulls his flannel shirt and t-shirt over his head, then stands to finish undressing.

My mouth falls open as I take in his incredible body. Muscles pop all over, and under the moonlight, I see the intricate web of scars on his arm and torso weaving in and out of his colorful tattoos.

"Roadside bomb," he says, tracing several of the scares. "Hurt like a motherfucker, but I survived."

"I can't imagine." I stand next to him, running my fingertips over his scars. I lower my mouth to his arm and kiss them.

Glen gasps and his body trembles. "Take off your clothes."

His voice is thick with desire, and I waste no time undressing. We're alone for miles.

We lie on the blanket, our kisses becoming passionate and urgent. I pull his body close to mine as one of his hands moves over my hips, then urges me to lie on my back. His fingers find my slick core, and my body quakes as they move quickly through my silken desire. My body arches into him, each stroke and tease of his fingers making my body hotter than our campfire.

I reach down and stroke his cock, biting my lip at how big he is now he's hard. His cock twitches as I touch him, and Glen groans, thrusting gently into my hand.

"I need to be inside you." Glen's voice is a husky whisper in my ear.

"Then come here, my darling."

I spread my legs, and Glen moves his powerful body over mine. He looks down at me, his eyes filled with a fierce love and tenderness. My hands move along his muscles, and I pull him into me. I squirm below him, unable to contain the hot desire that wants to burst from my body.

Glen guides himself into my hot core, and we cry out as he slides deep inside me. The cool mountain air nips at my skin, making my nipples stand at attention so tightly it's almost painful. Glen lowers his mouth and sucks at one and then the other, and I cry out again. He moves inside me, slowly at first, but then we find our rhythm and everything is touching and kissing and sucking and grinding into each other.

Each thrust of his cock pierces deeper inside me, and I know I've made the right decision. Happiness bursts in my body, and I wrap my legs and arms around his beautiful body, matching his rhythm and arching into him as he thrusts into me, our bodies frantically and hungrily moving as one.

"I love you, my beautiful Claudia." Glen looks me in the eyes, and my heart fills with more love than I ever knew it could hold.

"I love you, too." I gasp, pulling him deeper inside me. Our hearts and bodies fit together perfectly. "I'm so close," I moan into his mouth as he kisses me, our bodies moving faster and faster, the wool blanket scratching at my back. "I'm close."

My body thrashes with Glen's, my desire reaching a fever pitch as my orgasm builds, yearning to explode. Glen's eyes worship me as he matches my movements; faster, deeper, harder. My orgasm breaks over me in a hot explosion, lighting up my body like the stars in the sky. I hold onto him tightly as he pounds into my core, and then his body goes rigid as he comes.

Our bodies twitch together, and we hold each other tightly, our bodies touching from head to toe. We lie in silence as our hearts return to their normal rhythm. The owl hoots again as a pair of shooting stars streak across the clear night sky.

"I know what I'm going to call the refuge," I say, hugging Glen close. The cool air pricks at my skin, but Glen's body radiates heat, and I cling to him.

"What's that?"

"Shooting Star Dog Refuge."

"Actually, I have a suggestion. What do you think about Sweet Redemption Refuge? You are my sweet redemption and you will be providing a safe haven for dogs, until we can place them with others who need the redemption of a dog."

It's dark outside, but moonlight lights up the hopeful look on Glen's face, revealing how excited he is about this project, too. My life changed completely when Betty pushed me to work with Glen. I hate to admit it, but she's right – life is better when you share it with someone you love. Having a partner – in business and in life – when the refuge opens will be amazing.

"I think that's perfect, Glen. Sweet Redemption Refuge it is, then."

"We're going to build something amazing together." Glen kisses me gently and a wave of love leaves me breathless. I've always wanted to feel love like this and I feel so lucky to have found it.

"I look forward to it, my darling. I love you, too."

EPILOGUE

I stand at the edge of the woods and look at the refuge in front of me. Glen, Kirk, Waylon, and some friends of theirs are putting on the final touches on the barn, now. They finished up the main house last week, and Glen and I moving in tonight. We have most of our things moved up here, but tonight will be our first official night together in the refuge.

Seeing the refuge take shape has been the greatest professional achievement of my life. I've been working for years to make this happen and my heart fills with a fierce pride.

Since the day I met Glen, my life has been a whirlwind. I had dreamed of starting the refuge for so long, that I had started to doubt it would ever happen. But with each renovation of the cabin – the floors, the walls, a new roof, new appliances, and a dog-proof fence around the entire property – my heart has overflowed with joy.

"We're almost there." Glen comes up beside me, running a bandana over his face to clean it up. He puts his strong arms

EPILOGUE

around my shoulders and kisses the top of my head. I lean against him and hug him tightly.

"It's really happening…" Glen holds me tighter as my voice chokes with emotion. Everyone working on this doesn't question why this project is so important to me, but Glen understands completely. Being able to save abandoned dogs, to give them a loving life and second chance, is everything.

"I will always support you, Claudia. Always."

"I know, my darling." I pull his head down to mine and give him a long kiss. "How much longer are they here?" I smile up at him, sliding my hand down so that it cups his butt. With this being our first night in the house, we've been looking forward to breaking in our new bed.

Glen raises his eyebrow at me and grins. "I'll join them and make sure it's done double-time."

I watch as Glen rejoins the other men. He directs them with ease, careful to make sure everything is built correctly and safely. A lot of these guys are also vets and some of them are from a motorcycle club that one of Waylon's business partners used to be a part of.

I'm still learning everything Waylon and his men are involved in, but it's pretty extensive. They're committed to preserving the land, but they also have numerous properties around the mountain. Some of them are rentals, like the one Glen and I stayed at that first time he brought me up here to see this place, but some of the cabins are safe houses. Waylon told me about one of his buddies, Harley who fights human trafficking and sometimes brings women up here while he deals with the miscreants who were exploiting them.

EPILOGUE

The men of King Mountain, and the friends Glen, Kirk, and Waylon have, they're all tough men, many of them rough around the edges and tattooed, and living on the edge of the law. At first, I was intimidated, but I've learned they are a tight-knit family and they are fiercely protective of each other and the people important in their lives. That now includes me.

"I thought I'd find you out here!" Colleen waves and I walk over to where she's parked outside the fence line. We've been getting to know each other and she's starting to feel like a sister to me.

"It's so good to see you!" I hug Colleen tightly. "You didn't have to come up here, you know."

"Nonsense. I wanted to see how the refuge was progressing. Last time I was up here, it was still falling apart." She pauses as she takes in how much everything has changed, smiling when she spots Kirk. "Besides, we've left Kirk Junior with my parents, and we're spending the weekend in one of the cabins up here." She grins and winks at me.

"Why don't we go into the main house, then? I've got a pitcher of iced tea in the new fridge."

∼

"Okay. This is where we are with the fundraiser planning," Colleen says, showing me her laptop. "These are the sponsors we've lined up."

I look at the list and my mouth falls open. The list is so long, she has to scroll down on her laptop screen. "How? This is more than I imagined!"

EPILOGUE

Colleen smiles and puts her hand on my arm. "It's what we do. Plus, Warrior Cares is committed to working with you, and we have a lot of contacts who are committed to supporting Warrior Cares. Antonia also sent over a list," Colleen pauses, switching between screens and pulling up a different document, "of grants you can apply for. This isn't something we can help you with, but she has contacts who can help you if you need it."

"Thank you so much, Colleen!" I give her a big hug, tears forming in my eyes. It was a gamble to get the renovations underway before the fundraiser, but Colleen and Antonia assured me the fundraiser would be a success. Yet looking at the sponsors they've lined up and what she's described as a lowball estimate of what they'll bring in, it's beyond my wildest dreams.

"You're part of the family now." Colleen hugs me back tightly. "People love to give money away. Antonia and I just help those people find people who deserve it – like you."

∼

"How was the meeting with Colleen?" Glen sits with me on the porch, sipping iced tea as we watch the sunset, as Mutt, Midnight, and Daisy chase each other in the fenced yard. The men are all finished up and it's just us now.

"She is truly amazing." I fill Glen in on everything she shared with me and he whistles.

"Kirk said she was a force of nature. Sounds like everything is working out alright."

"Everything is working out perfect. You're a big part of that, Glen. I love you, my darling. Thank you for being so supportive." I kiss Glen and joy fills every cell of my body. I feel loved, like no dream is too big to achieve.

"I mean it when I say you are my redemption, Claudia." Glen looks at me intently and my body vibrates with emotion. Even though he's told me a million times how much I mean to him, part of my brain still has a hard time accepting it. Though I think that's why he tells me so often, because he understands how long I went feeling like I was alone in the world. "Ain't nothing going to ever stop me from doing everything I can to support you and the dogs, or to help you achieve anything else you want in life. I'm fully committed to you. My body and soul are yours."

Glen's kiss starts gentle, but it quickly deepens with pure passion. Glen slips his hand under the bottom of my shirt and I giggle at the tickle of his fingers against my skin. I lean into his hand, eager to feel his naked body next to mine.

"I think we need to bring the dogs in." My voice is breathy and jagged, my words coming in short bursts. Glen's mouth is on my neck as his hands work to undo the button of my jeans. My core is already hot and slick for him, eager to feel his thick cock pushing into me and giving me a pleasure only he can.

Glen pulls away from me, standing up and whistling for the dogs. All three of them come at his command, Mutt leading the way. Once I taught Glen how to train Mutt, Glen was a natural. Mutt obeys all his commands and is an excellent companion for him. Glen says he loves all the dogs equally, but I know Mutt holds a special place in his heart.

We all go into the cabin and the dogs circle around their beds, before plopping down and stretching out.

EPILOGUE

"Come here, my beautiful Claudia. Let's get you out of those clothes and into our bed." Glen grins at me, his eyes hungrily raking over my body, lingering on my hips and breasts.

I always used to think that having extra curves was unattractive to men, but Glen worships my curves. I never have to suck in my stomach with him or pretend to think a salad is satisfying. He shows me every night how much he loves my wide hips and heavy breasts, and it makes me love him even more. He loves me, completely and utterly as I am, just like I love him.

My fingers trace the tattoos and scars on his arms, then Glen lifts my shirt over my head as I squirm out of my jeans. He sometimes thinks the scars make him a lesser man, but I think the scars make him more beautiful. Through each other, we've learned we can't hide from our past, but we need to embrace who we are and learn to move forward. It is my greatest privilege that my journey forward is with Glen.

As we get into bed and our bodies merge into one, I know that Glen is my redemption, too. I will never let him go.

~

Thank you so much for reading *Sweet Redemption*!

*This book is part of the **Heart of a Wounded Hero** series. The Heart of the Wounded Hero series was created to pay tribute to and raise awareness of our wounded heroes. Each of the over eighty authors involved have contributed time, money, and stories to the cause. These love stories are inspiring and uplifting, showing the sacrifice of our veterans but also giving them the happily ever after they deserve. By increasing awareness through our books, we believe we can in a small part help the wounded heroes that have*

EPILOGUE

sacrificed so much. Thank you for reading! To catch up on the full series, please visit:

https://www.amazon.com/dp/B09YMQ471K

If you enjoyed this book, please leave a review on Amazon, Goodreads, or Bookbub! Thank you!

Do you want to read Kirk and Colleen's love story? They're featured in *Falling for Her Curves*.

https://www.amazon.com/dp/B09VXNFPXJ

Want to stay up to date on new releases, sales, and freebies! Join my newsletter!

http://eepurl.com/dh59Xr

For more books by Lana Love, please visit my Amazon page at:

https://www.amazon.com/Lana-Love/e/B078KKRB1T/

or visit my website at:

https://www.loveheartbooks.com